# Angela Nicely

ALAN MACDONALD ILLUSTRATED BY DAVID ROBERTS

Look out for the
next *Angela Nicely*
book coming soon:
Queen Bee!

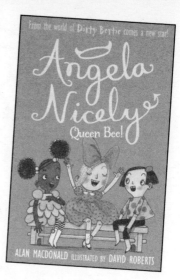

Also by Alan MacDonald and
David Roberts – *Dirty Bertie*!

| | | |
|---|---|---|
| Worms! | Mud! | Snow! |
| Fleas! | Germs! | Pong! |
| Pants! | Loo! | Pirate! |
| Burp! | Fetch! | Scream! |
| Yuck! | Fangs! | Toothy! |
| Crackers! | Kiss! | Dinosaur! |
| Bogeys! | Ouch! | My Joke Book |

# Contents

# Chapter 1

It was nine o'clock on Monday morning. Angela sat in the hall next to Laura and Maisie. They were waiting for assembly to start.

"Good morning, children," said Miss Skinner.

"GOOD MOR-NING, MISS SKIN-NER!" chanted the children.

Miss Skinner's gaze swept over the rows of faces like a cold wind.

"Jemma Bumford, stop fidgeting. Jimmy Wallop, turn round. Bertie, wipe your nose ... not on Darren!"

Angela sat up straight and gazed at Miss Skinner. Her mouth fell open. There was something different about the Head Teacher today. *Her hair!* She always wore her hair in a bun that looked like a brown ring doughnut. But today her hair hung loose in frizzy curls. RED curls! Angela stared. How could it have grown longer and curlier? And changed colour? It was impossible. Unless... Angela's eyes almost popped out of her head. MISS SKINNER WAS WEARING A WIG!

8

Angela nudged Laura. "Look what she's wearing!" she whispered.

Laura looked. "Sandals," she said.

"No, on her head!" hissed Angela.

Laura looked again. Miss Skinner wasn't wearing anything on her head except...

"OH!" gasped Laura. Miss Skinner's hair had had some sort of makeover.

"See?" hissed Angela. "It's a—"

"ANGELA NICELY!" Miss Skinner's voice made Angela jump. "Is there something you want to share with us?"

Angela gulped. "No, Miss," she mumbled.

"Speak up," said Miss Skinner. "It's obviously important."

Angela shook her head, her cheeks burning. She could feel everyone staring at her. Luckily, Miss Skinner went back to what she was saying.

After assembly Angela and her friends headed back to class.

"How come it's always me that gets in trouble?" grumbled Angela.

"You were talking," said Laura.

"So were you," argued Angela.

"Anyway, what were you whispering about?" asked Maisie.

Angela stopped dead. "You mean you didn't notice?" she said.

Maisie looked at her blankly.

"Miss Skinner IS WEARING A WIG," said Angela, spelling it out.

Maisie snorted. "She's not!"

"SHE IS! It's so obvious!"

Maisie looked at her. "Angela! You are such a fibber!"

11

"It's a wig!" insisted Angela.

"It isn't!"

"Is!" said Angela, throwing up her hands in despair. "Look," she said, "before her hair was short and brown, and she had it in a bun. Now it's long, curly and RED! It *has* to be a wig."

Maisie rolled her eyes. "Angela, you are raving barmy bonkers!"

Angela sighed. Maisie was her second best friend, but she could be really annoying sometimes.

"It *definitely* is," said Angela.

Maisie gave her a look. "Okay," she said. "Prove it."

"Right, I will!" said Angela.

Laura frowned. "How? How can you prove it?"

Angela hadn't thought about that. She couldn't exactly go up to Miss Skinner and say, "Please, Miss, can you show us your wig?" Teachers went mad when you said things like that. Even if you were just helpfully pointing out a spot on their nose. No, she would have to think of a plan. Maisie always thought she knew best, but this time Angela would prove her wrong.

# Chapter 2

By lunchtime, Angela had the perfect plan. Miss Skinner spent most of the time in her office, so all they had to do was keep watch. Sooner or later they'd catch her without her wig. Angela explained her plan to Laura and Maisie as they headed outside after lunch.

"Keep watch?" said Laura. "How?"

"Through her window," said Angela.

Laura looked worried. "But what if we get caught?"

"We won't," said Angela. She never got caught – well, almost never.

"And how will we catch her without her wig?" objected Maisie.

"She has to take it off sometime," said Angela. "I bet it gets itchy. She probably takes it off when no one's about and hangs it on the door."

Laura tried to imagine it. Maybe Miss Skinner had different wigs – one for each day of the week?

Maisie shook her head. "It'll never work."

"It will," said Angela. "Come on!"

A few minutes later they slipped past Mr Weakly, who was on duty, and headed round the back of the school. Miss Skinner's office looked out over the playing field. Mr Grouch, the caretaker, kept his compost heap here and it was STRICTLY OUT OF BOUNDS. It was piled high with smelly slops and leftovers from lunch.

"Pooh!" grumbled Laura. "It stinks!"

Angela edged past the compost heap and stood on tiptoe.

"Well? Can you see her?" whispered Maisie, hanging back.

"The window's too high!" said Angela. "You'll have to give me a lift."

Maisie crouched down and Angela clambered on to her shoulders. From there she had the perfect view. Miss Skinner was working at her desk, with her back towards the window.

"She's in there," reported Angela.

"What about her hair?" asked Laura.

"She's still wearing it."

"Told you," said Maisie. "It's not a wig!" She groaned. "Hurry up, Angela! You're heavy!"

"Keep still," hissed Angela. "I can't see if you keep wobbling."

COMPOST

It was just a matter of time. Any minute now Miss Skinner would remove her wig to scratch her head.

Then it happened. Miss Skinner stood up, stretched and turned round. She caught sight of a pale face staring at her through the window.

"ARGHHHHH!" she screamed.

"WAAAAHHH!" yelled Angela, losing her balance.

Miss Skinner saw the face vanish from sight and heard a thump. She hurried to the window and pulled it up. "ANGELA NICELY!" she thundered.

Angela sat up. Luckily, something had broken her fall. Unluckily, it was Mr Grouch's pongy compost heap. She was covered in lumpy custard and mouldy cabbage.

"EWWWW!" she cried, crawling out.

"It serves you right," snapped Miss Skinner. "What were you doing?"

"Just ... erm ... looking for something," stammered Angela.

"For what?"

"My PE kit," said Angela.

COMPOST

"Don't tell lies!" cried Miss Skinner. "You were spying on me! What for?"

Angela looked at the ground. She didn't have an explanation, at least not one she could tell Miss Skinner.

"Very well," said Miss Skinner. "Clean yourself up. Then you can stand outside my office for the rest of lunchtime."

She caught sight of Maisie and Laura trying to sneak away. "As for you two, I shall be speaking to your teacher."

WHAM! The window slammed shut.

Maisie glared at Angela. "I told you it wouldn't work. Now you've got us all in trouble."

"What about me? I'm all stinky," moaned Angela. "What's my mum going to say?"

# Chapter 3

Angela stood outside Miss Skinner's office feeling sorry for herself. She was in big trouble with Miss Skinner and she was still no nearer to proving that the Head was wearing a wig. She'd done her best to wipe off the tomato and custard stains, but she couldn't do anything about the smell.

Tiffany Charmers walked past. "Oh dear, Angela. In trouble again?" she smiled.

Angela stuck out her tongue.

DRRRING!

The bell went for the end of lunch

Miss Skinner came out of her office. "Well, Angela," she said. "I hope you've had time to think about your behaviour. It is very rude to spy on people."

"Yes, Miss. Sorry," said Angela.

"I don't want to catch you at my window again, or near Mr Grouch's compost heap. Is that clear?"

"I promise," said Angela. "It smells."

Miss Skinner sniffed. "So it would seem. Now get back to your class."

Angela hurried off. As she passed

the staffroom, she saw Mr Grouch
inside hoovering. The caretaker was as
grumpy as an ogre and hated children
bothering him. But Angela had seen
something that had given her an idea.

"Hi, Mr Grouch!" she said, smiling
up at him.

The caretaker turned off the Hoover.

"What do you want?" he glared.

"I just wondered what you're doing,"
said Angela.

"What does it look like?" snapped
Mr Grouch.

He went to turn the Hoover back on,
but Angela was inspecting it.

"What does this do?" she asked.

Mr Grouch sighed. Schools would
be much better without children, he
thought, especially children who asked

annoying questions. All the same,
the Hoover was new and he enjoyed
showing it off.

"This is the Super Suction Arm," he
said. "Stand back."

He turned on the Hoover.

VWOOOOOOM!

A scrap of paper
vanished inside.

"See?" said Mr Grouch. "Dust, fluff, paper – it all gets sucked in here."

"Wow!" said Angela, impressed. "Can it pick up anything? Even hair?"

"Hair? Yes, of course."

"Can I have a go?" asked Angela.

"No, you can't," snapped the caretaker. "Now go and bother someone else."

Angela tripped off down the corridor, smiling to herself. A Super Suction Arm might be just what she needed...

Back in class, everyone looked up when Angela came in.

"Eww! What's that smell?" chanted the Payne twins.

"Pooh! Is that you, Angela?" mocked Tiffany Charmers, holding her nose.

Angela ignored them and sat down.

"What did Miss Skinner say?" whispered Laura.

Angela shrugged. "She just told me not to spy on her."

"Well, I hope you're satisfied," said Maisie. "*Now* do you admit I'm right?"

"No," replied Angela. "It's a wig and I know how to prove it."

Maisie groaned. The trouble with Angela was she never knew when she was beaten.

# Chapter 4

At half past three, the bell went.
Children hurried out of the classrooms
and swarmed through the main door.

Angela poked her head out of the
cloakroom to check no one was about.

"Can't we go home?" whined Laura.

"My mum will be cross if I'm late,"
moaned Maisie.

But Angela took no notice. She hurried over to Mr Grouch's cleaning cupboard and dragged out the Hoover.

"You can't take that!" cried Laura.

"I'm only borrowing it," said Angela.

"What for?" asked Maisie.

"To prove I'm right," said Angela.

She dragged the Hoover down the corridor to Miss Skinner's office and knocked on the door. There was no answer. She peeped in.

"ANGELA!" wailed Laura.

"It's okay, she's not there," said Angela. "Come on!"

They tiptoed inside. Laura looked around anxiously. They were definitely not meant to be in here. Angela had landed them in trouble once already today. Miss Skinner would go potty if she found them snooping in her room.

"Let's go!" begged Maisie. "I don't care who was right."

"I'm right," insisted Angela. "It's a wig and this will prove it."

"A Hoover?" said Laura.

"That's right. Watch this," said Angela, switching it on.

Unfortunately, the Super Suction Arm was pointing at Miss Skinner's desk.

VWOOOOM!

A pile of papers took off and were gobbled up in an instant. Paperclips, pencils and pens vanished into the Hoover with a rattle. Some yellow tulips shot out of a vase and were swallowed whole.

"STOP!" cried Laura. "Turn it off!"

Angela pressed the "OFF" button.
She looked round the Head's office.
The room looked like it had been hit by
a hurricane.

"Ooops!" said Angela. "Quick, help
me clear up."

But it was too late. Footsteps were coming down the corridor.

"HIDE!" hissed Angela.

The door opened and Miss Skinner walked in. She stood there for a moment, speechless. Then she caught sight of a pink bow behind her desk.

"ANGELA!" she yelled.

Three faces peeped into view.

"It wasn't my fault," said Angela in a small voice.

"Then whose fault was it?" stormed Miss Skinner.

The three girls got to their feet.

"It was Angela's idea," said Maisie.

"We were only trying to help," mumbled Laura.

"Yes," nodded Angela. "I just wanted to clean your room to show I was sorry."

"Clean it? You've destroyed it!" cried Miss Skinner. "And where did you get that Hoover?"

"I borrowed it," said Angela. She glanced at Miss Skinner's hair. If only she could get the Head to bend over the Super Suction Arm, her plan would work. But how? Then she had an idea.

"I think it's broken!" she said suddenly.

"What?" said Miss Skinner.

"The Hoover. I think there's something's stuck in here. Look."

"It better not be broken," said Miss

Skinner, peering into it. "It's brand new."

Angela took a deep breath – it was now or never. She turned the Hoover on.

VWOOOOM!

"ARGHHH!" squawked Miss Skinner. The Super Suction Arm had got hold of her hair and was trying to eat it. Laura and Maisie watched in horror as the Head struggled to escape.

"TURN IT OFF!" she screeched.

Angela switched it off. There was a long silence, filled only by Miss Skinner's heavy breathing. Her frazzled hair stood on end as if she'd had an electric shock. One thing was certain, though – it was definitely real.

"Oh," gulped Angela.

"Told you," muttered Maisie.

Miss Skinner took a deep breath. She had spent a small fortune on her new hairstyle. "GET OUT!" she bellowed. "ALL OF YOU – OUT!"

34

"Well?" said Maisie, when they'd finally stopped running. "Now do you admit it? I was right all along."

"Okay, okay," sighed Angela. "You were right." She lowered her voice. "But you know Mr Weakly?"

"Yes?" said Laura and Maisie.

"Now he *definitely* wears a wig."

# Chapter 1

Every Monday morning Miss Darling's class met on the carpet for News Time. And this morning Angela had really exciting news: her family was getting a dog. It was a fact, although she hadn't told her parents yet. But the trouble with News Time was that all the class wanted to speak. If you went, "Ooh, ooh, Miss," or tugged at Miss Darling's skirt, she wouldn't pick you.

"Well," said their teacher, smiling. "Who has some news today?"

Every hand shot in the air.

"Laura, what's your news?" asked Miss Darling.

"I went to the park yesterday," said Laura.

"Did you? Lovely!" said Miss Darling. "William?"

"I cut my knee and it bled on the carpet," said William.

"Oh, you poor thing! Who else?"

Angela tried to catch Miss Darling's eye. It had to be her turn next – if she didn't speak soon she would burst.

Miss Darling's gaze rested on her for

a moment, before moving on.

"Tiffany, what's your news?"

Angela's arm flopped down. Why did goody-goody Tiffany always get picked? Tiffany was top of the class and teacher's pet.

"I'm going to be a model," she boasted, hugging herself.

"A model?" said Miss Darling. "Really?"

Tiffany nodded. "It's for Poppets' catalogue."

"How exciting!" said Miss Darling.

"I know," said Tiffany. "Mummy's taking me to the casting on Saturday."

"Ah. So it isn't definite yet?" said Miss Darling.

"No, but they're bound to pick me," said Tiffany. "Mummy says I'd be perfect."

"Well, that *is* thrilling news!" said Miss Darling. "I think we should all give Tiffany a big clap."

Everyone clapped while Tiffany glowed with pride.

"Right, back to your seats and get out your books," said Miss Darling.

Angela threw back her head. It was so unfair! She hadn't said a word while Tiffany had hogged all the time. It was the same every week. Last Monday it was Tiffany's ballet exam and the week before that she boasted she was getting a pony.

Angela slumped into her seat. Who cared about being a model anyway? Of course, you'd probably get amazing clothes to wear. And have your picture taken all the time, which would be okay. And lots of models were rich and famous. Hang on... Angela had second thoughts. Actually she wouldn't mind being a model – and she'd be miles better at it than Toffee-Nosed Tiffany!

She leaned over to Laura. "I bet I could be a model," she whispered.

"You couldn't," said Laura.

"Why not?"

"Because you have to be chosen like Tiffany," said Laura.

"She hasn't been chosen yet," said Angela. "And you never know, they might choose someone else."

That evening Angela brought up the subject over supper.

"You'll never guess what Tiffany is doing," she said.

Mrs Nicely rolled her eyes. "Something marvellous, I expect."

"She's going to be a model!" said Angela.

Mrs Nicely's mouth fell open. "SHE ISN'T!"

"She is," said Angela. "In Poppets' catalogue. She told us in News Time."

"Good for Tiffany," said Mr Nicely.

His wife shot him a look. "I bet it's her mother's idea," she said. "Mrs Charmers never tires of telling me how wonderful Tiffany is."

Angela squashed a pea with her fork. "The casting's on Saturday," she said.

Mrs Nicely looked at her. "You mean it's like an audition? Anyone can go along?"

Angela shrugged. "I think so."

"Right then, you are going too," decided Mrs Nicely. "If Tiffany can be a model, then I'm certain you can."

Mr Nicely frowned. "Is that a good idea?" he said. "Isn't Angela a bit young to be a model?"

His wife glared at him. "Are you saying she's not as pretty as Tiffany?"

"No, of course not."

"Well then, that's settled," said Mrs Nicely. "I think Angela would make a wonderful model."

Angela smiled. She imagined her picture in Poppets' catalogue. It would be worth it just to see Tiffany's face.

# Chapter 2

On Saturday morning Angela and her
mum set off for the casting. When they
arrived they were directed to a room
crowded with small girls and their
parents.

"Goodness!" huffed Mrs Nicely. "I
had no idea there'd be so many people."

After hours of waiting, Angela's
name was finally called.

"If you'd like to go through," said the secretary, pointing to a door.

They found themselves in a smaller room where a girl was waiting with her mum. She had her back turned, but even before she looked round Angela recognized Tiffany Charmers. She was wearing new red shoes and ribbons in her hair.

Angela Nicely

Angela sat down beside her. "Hello, Tiffany."

"Hello, Angela," said Tiffany. "What are you doing here?"

"Same as you."

Tiffany's mouth twitched. "You want to be a model? That's so sweet!"

Angela glared. "I stand as much chance as you."

Tiffany looked her over. "Is that what you're wearing?" she said.

"Yes," said Angela. "It's my favourite dress."

"Never mind," said Tiffany with a sigh. "I'm sure it won't matter."

Angela bit her lip. Tiffany was the most annoying person in the universe. Even worse, Angela had to listen to Mrs Charmers singing her praises.

"Don't you think Tiffany looks *adorable*?" she was saying.

"Er, yes, I suppose so," said Mrs Nicely.

"And she's so talented!" Mrs Charmers went on. "In her ballet class you just can't keep your eyes off her…"

"Angela's very talented too," said Mrs Nicely.

As the two mothers chatted, Tiffany reached into her bag and brought out a Twizzle bar. "Do you want some chocolate?" she asked Angela.

Angela stared. "Is this a trick?"

"Of course not, silly," said Tiffany.
"I'm just not that hungry and it'll melt
in my bag. But if you don't—"

Angela grabbed the Twizzle bar.
There was no sense in letting good
chocolate go to waste. Better eat it
quickly. Yum! Twizzle bars were
her favourite.

Just then the door opened and a
woman came in.

"Hi, my name's Melanie," she said.
"Sorry to keep you— OH!"

She stared in horror at Angela.

"ANGELA!" screeched Mrs Nicely.
"Look at you!"

Angela looked up. She had chocolate
smeared round her mouth and a dark
splodge on her dress.

Mrs Nicely leaped up and began
dabbing at Angela's face with a hanky.

"It wasn't my fault!" cried Angela.
"Tiffany gave it to me!"

"Really, Angela, don't try and blame
Tiffany," snapped Mrs Nicely.

"Yes, ANG-ER-LA!" said Tiffany
with a smirk.

50

Angela stuck out her tongue, which was a mistake because it was sticky with chocolate.

Melanie glanced at her watch. "Perhaps you should get Angela cleaned up," she said. "In the meantime, we'll see Tiffany."

Tiffany stood up, patted her curly hair and gave Angela a look of triumph.

# Chapter 3

By the time Angela joined them in the studio, Tiffany was posing for photos. She sat, beaming at the camera.

"That's super," said the photographer.

"Perfect," said Melanie. "So, what do you like doing, Tiffany?"

"I like ballet!" sang Tiffany.

"Great, can you show us some steps?"

Tiffany jumped up and pointed her toes. She sprang in the air, spun round and landed gracefully.

Mrs Charmers clapped loudly. "Beautiful, darling!"

Angela had to hand it to her, Tiffany knew how to put on a show.

Then it was Angela's turn.

"Remember, don't slouch and don't forget to smile," whispered her mum.

Angela nodded. She sat up very straight and smiled her widest smile.

"Just try to relax," said the photographer.

"I am relaxed," said Angela, showing her teeth.

"Okay," said Melanie. "What do you enjoy doing, Angela?"

"Loads of things," said Angela. "Watching TV, playing with my friends, standing on my head…"

"You can stand on your head?"

"It's easy!" said Angela, jumping up. She flipped over with her legs in the air. Her dress flopped over her head.

Mrs Nicely groaned and covered her eyes.

A few days later, a letter arrived in the post. Mrs Nicely opened it as she came into the kitchen.

"ARGHHHHHH!" she screamed. "You got it! Poppets want you to model for the catalogue!"

Angela jumped up and did a dance round the kitchen. To be honest, she was a bit surprised – what with the chocolate stains and everything – but maybe Poppets needed a model that could stand on their head…?

# Chapter 4

At last the day of the photo shoot
came and a minibus arrived to collect
them. The shoot was taking place at
the seaside and Angela could hardly
wait. The only bad news was that
Tiffany was one of the other models.

As soon as they arrived, they were
shown into a beach hut to change into

their outfits. Melanie took down a dress from the clothes rail. It was pink with a white lacy collar. Angela stared at it longingly.

"Let's see," said Melanie. "I think this one is for…"

Angela stood on tiptoe.

"…Tiffany!" said Melanie.

Angela threw up her hands. Why was it *always* Tiffany?

"And these are for you, Angela," said Melanie. She handed over a pair of stripey dungaree shorts.

Tiffany put on the dress and twirled around, admiring herself in the mirror.

"What do you think, Angela?" she cooed.

Angela shrugged. "It's okay."

She frowned at herself in the mirror

as she buttoned up the dungarees.
The stripes were bright red and green.
She looked like a deckchair.

Tiffany giggled. "Oh Angela! They
suit you!"

Angela scowled and stomped off to
find her mum.

"Oh. Dungarees," said Mrs Nicely. "Never mind, models have to wear what they're given. Now remember, *don't* get them dirty. No sweets or ice creams, just STAY PUT until you're called."

Angela sighed. Being a model wasn't half as much fun as she'd thought. What was the point of coming to the seaside if you couldn't go in the sea? The sun was out, the mums were having coffee and the other models were posing by the beach huts. Only Angela was STAYING PUT.

She looked round and spotted Tiffany standing on a towel to avoid getting sandy. Suddenly, an idea crept into Angela's head. What if Tiffany got her precious dress dirty? Or wet?

Then *she'd* be the one in trouble for a change. It would serve her right for playing that sneaky chocolate trick.

"Aren't you hot, Tiffany?" Angela asked, going over.

"I don't mind," said Tiffany.

Angela heaved a sigh. "I bet the sea's lovely and cool."

Tiffany shook her head. "We're not allowed. Melanie said we have to stay on the beach."

"We will," said Angela, setting off towards the sea. "It's all the beach."

Tiffany glanced back at the others. It *was* very hot and the photos *were* taking ages. Besides, she was only going to take a look.

Down at the water, Angela started to take off her sandals.

"ANGELA! YOU CAN'T!" cried
Tiffany.

"It's okay. I'm only going for a
paddle," said Angela.

Tiffany watched enviously as Angela
waded into the water.

"Come on! It's lovely!" she called.

"But what about my dress?" wailed Tiffany.

"Hold it up!" said Angela.

Tiffany hung back. But the water did look tempting. And if anyone saw them she'd blame it on Angela. She took off her shoes and socks and hitched up her dress.

Angela waded out a little deeper and looked back. Tiffany was dipping her toes daintily in the shallows. She'd never get wet like that.

"COME ON!" cried Angela. "It's not deep. Look!" She kicked her foot. Oops! Her dungarees had got a tiny bit wet. She'd better be careful…

KERSPLOSH!

Suddenly a giant wave swept right over her.

"UGH! OHHHHHH!" cried Angela,
gasping for breath.

"OH, ANGELA!" Tiffany bent over,
helpless with laughter.

But Angela didn't see the funny
side. She splodged out of the sea and
stood on the sand, dripping like an
ice-cream cone. This wasn't supposed
to happen! It was Tiffany who was
meant to get wet!

Just then their mums came hurrying down the beach with Melanie.

"Tiffany! Darling! Are you all right?" panted Mrs Charmers.

"I'm fine," said Tiffany. "It's Angela!"

"ANGELA!" groaned Mrs Nicely.

"It wasn't my fault," cried Angela. "I only went for a paddle, but a big wave splooshed me!"

*Angela Nicely*

Mrs Nicely turned to Melanie. "I am so sorry," she said.

Melanie shook her head. "Never mind, it can't be helped. But she can't be in the photos like that."

Angela's face fell. It had all turned out wrong. Now only Tiffany's picture would be in the catalogue.

"Isn't there anything else she could wear?" asked Mrs Nicely.

Melanie frowned. "There's the mermaid costume," she said.

"MERMAID COSTUME?" gasped Angela.

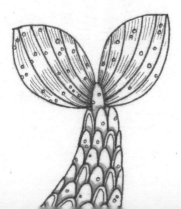

Ten minutes later Angela had changed into her new outfit. The photographer lined up the other models with Tiffany on the end. Then she got them to hold Angela. She was wearing a silver tail and a huge grin.

"Right then," said the photographer. "Everyone shout 'ICE CREAM!'"

"ICE CREAM!" they yelled.

CLICK!

Angela thought it was the best photo of them all – in fact, it ended up on the cover of Poppets' catalogue!

Tiffany was furious. But as Angela said to her, "We can't all be supermodels!"

# Chapter 1

"ARRGHH! URRRRRGH!"

Angela hurried upstairs. Strange noises were coming from her parents' bedroom. It sounded like her mum was having a tooth out.

"ANGELA! Can you come here a moment!" yelled Mrs Nicely.

Uh oh. Surely her mum wasn't still

cross about her painting the cat's claws? Nervously, she poked her head round the bedroom door. Mrs Nicely was standing in front of the mirror, wrestling with her dress.

"Did you call me?" asked Angela.

"Yes, I can't seem to zip up this dress," huffed her mum.

Was that all? Angela breathed a sigh of relief. She took hold of the zip and pulled. It didn't move.

"It won't go," she said.

"Don't be silly. Try harder," said Mrs Nicely.

Angela climbed on to the bed to get a better grip. She tugged. She heaved. She panted and pulled. Finally she flopped back on the bed, out of breath. "It's no good, it won't budge."

Mrs Nicely frowned. "It was fine last time I wore it. Maybe it's shrunk."

"Or maybe you got bigger," suggested Angela.

"Bigger?" Mrs Nicely's eyebrows shot up. "Do you mean FATTER?"

Angela prodded her mum's tummy. "You're not fat, just a bit squidgy," she grinned.

"SQUIDGY?" screeched Mrs Nicely.

Angela rolled her eyes. Parents could be so touchy. They were always saying that she should tell the truth, but when she did they hit the roof!

Mrs Nicely turned sideways, inspecting herself in the mirror. She reached behind and yanked the zip up.

RRRRRIPPP!

"ARGHHHHHHHHHHHH!"

Angela jumped off the bed and hurried to her room. When her mum was in a bad mood it was best to stay out of the way. Her dad usually hid in the shed.

Half an hour later, Angela came downstairs. She could hear drawers crashing and banging in the kitchen.

"What's going on?" she asked, peeping round the door.

"Found it!" cried her mum, waving a piece of paper.

"Found what?" Angela's dad looked up from his newspaper.

Mrs Nicely handed over a leaflet.

*Get into shape! Take a spa break at Bracegirdle Hall!* it said.

"A spa break?" said Angela. "What's that?"

"It's a sort of healthy holiday," explained her mum. "I might book it for this weekend."

"Can I come?" pleaded Angela. She loved holidays.

"I don't see why not," said her mum.

"YAHOOOO!" whooped Angela.

Mrs Nicely sighed. "Please don't do that, Angela. It gives me a headache."

Her husband looked doubtful. "Are you sure it's a good idea?" he asked. "It's not really for children."

"Of course it is," said Mrs Nicely. "There'll be sun loungers, hot tubs, a swimming pool…"

"A swimming pool?" cried Angela excitedly. "Is it like Splash City?"

Bertie, the boy next door, had told her about Splash City. It had six slides and the Rocky Rapids River Ride. Bertie said it was too dangerous for girls, but Angela wasn't scared of anything.

"Something like that," said Mrs Nicely. "Anyway, I'm sure there'll be plenty to do."

"Will they have pancakes for breakfast?" asked Angela.

"I expect so."

"YAHOOOOOOO!" yelled Angela. "Sorry. I mean yahoo."

# Chapter 2

On Friday evening Angela and her
mum arrived at Bracegirdle Hall and
headed for reception. Everything
was gleaming and spotlessly white.
A woman walked past dressed in a
white tunic and trousers.

"Mum," whispered Angela. "I think
it's a hospital."

"Don't be silly, Angela," said Mrs
Nicely. "You wait, by Sunday we'll be
the picture of health – and I shall fit into
my dress."

Just then, a door swung open and a
gigantic woman marched in. She had
heavy eyebrows, huge arms and a hairy
mole on her chin.

"Welcome to Bracegirdle Hall,"
she barked. "I am Miss Bullock, your
personal trainer. I will be in charge of
your programme."

"Oh, er, lovely," said Mrs Nicely.

"Can we see the swimming pool?"
begged Angela, pulling on her mum's
hand. She couldn't wait to zoom down
the Rocky Rapids River Ride.

Miss Bullock waved a beefy arm.
"Plenty of time for that later. First, have

you any forbidden goods in your bags? Chocolate, crisps, cakes – nasty things like that?"

"Er, I don't think so," said Mrs Nicely.

Miss Bullock gave a snort and unzipped Mrs Nicely's bag. She put in her hand and seized a packet of ginger creams.

"What do you call this?" she cried.

"Oh, those – they're for my daughter," stammered Mrs Nicely.

"They are not!" said Angela. "Ginger creams are *your* favourite."

"Quiet, Angela," snapped Mrs Nicely, going pink.

But Miss Bullock hadn't finished yet. She grabbed Angela's bag. There was a fudge bar in the pocket. Miss Bullock pounced on it.

"HA! Chocolate!" she cried. "Strictly against the rules."

"But it's mine," argued Angela.

Miss Bullock shoved the bar in her pocket. "Horrible sugary muck. I will take care of it," she said. "Right, let me show you to your room. Lights out at 10 p.m. I'll meet you in reception tomorrow morning at 8 a.m. sharp, dressed for exercise."

The next morning, Angela and her mum waited by reception, their stomachs rumbling. Breakfast had been a measly bowl of muesli.

"When do we go in the swimming pool?" asked Angela.

"Soon," said Mrs Nicely. "I expect they want to give us tea and a tour of the hall first."

Miss Bullock arrived, wearing a running vest and tiny shorts. She didn't look dressed for tea.

"Good," she said, rubbing her hands. "We'll begin with a light jog."

"A jog?" said Mrs Nicely. She hadn't jogged since she was at school.

"But it's raining," protested Angela.

80

"Pah! A spot of rain will do you good," said Miss Bullock. She bounded off down the drive. "Come on, keep up!"

An hour later, Angela and her mum staggered up a steep, grassy bank. They were soaking wet, muddy and exhausted.

"No dawdling!" yelled Miss Bullock.

"I can't go any further," panted Angela.

"Nor me," gasped Mrs Nicely.

Miss Bullock looked at her watch.

"COME ON! We'll miss lunch!"

Angela ran. Her mum broke into a feeble trot. At the bottom of the hill was a large muddy puddle.

SPLAT!

Angela skidded and sat down with a squelch. Her mum slid down the hill and fell on top of her. They slipped and slopped around like two hippos in a mud bath.

Miss Bullock rolled her eyes. "Get up, the pair of you!" she barked. "Last one back to the hall does twenty press-ups!"

# Chapter 3

After a quick shower they hurried down
for lunch. Angela was so hungry she
thought she could eat three whole bowls
of spaghetti. She sat down. A waitress
set down two plates in front of them.

Angela stared at her plate. Three
tiny slices of beetroot sat on a bed of
shredded carrot.

"I can't eat this!" cried Angela. "I hate beetroot!"

"Don't be so fussy," said her mum. "It's good for you."

Angela chewed a bit of carrot and pulled a face.

"Excuse me," her mum asked the waitress. "Isn't there anything else?"

"Oh yes, there's dessert," said the waitress. "Low fat yoghurt or half an apple."

*Half* an apple? Angela slumped back in her chair. Were they trying to starve them to death? This was meant to be a holiday! Well, holidays had chips and ice creams – Bracegirdle Hall was more like a prison.

"Can't we go home?" she moaned.

"Certainly not," said Mrs Nicely.

"Exercise and healthy eating will do us the world of good."

Angela leaned forward. "I know where we can get lots of exercise," she said.

"Where?" said her mum.

"Splash City! They've got six slides and—"

"NO, Angela!" cried Mrs Nicely. "We are staying and that's final."

After lunch, Miss Bullock had a special treat for them. Their next session was in the swimming pool.

*This is more like it*, thought Angela. At last she could have some fun!

She raced out of the changing room and stopped dead. There had to be some mistake. Where were the slides, the Rocky Rapids and the Turbo Twister?

Miss Bullock blew her whistle. "Right, jump in. Six lengths front crawl!"

"But I can't do crawl," Angela moaned.

Miss Bullock rolled her eyes. "What can you do?"

"Doggy paddle," said Angela. "And only if I'm wearing arm bands."

Miss Bullock thrust a foam float into her hands. "Get going," she ordered.

*Angela Nicely*

After an hour of swimming lengths,
Angela and her mum staggered back to
the changing room.

Mrs Nicely flopped on to a bench.
"No more, please!" she gasped.

"I'm starving," moaned Angela. "Can
we get some crisps?"

"Crisps aren't allowed," said Mrs Nicely.

"What about
doughnuts?"

"No!"

"Iced buns?"
said Angela.

Mrs Nicely
covered her ears.
"Angela will
you *please*
stop talking
about food!"

Angela looked at the clock on the wall. It was hours till dinner time. She'd never last out. If only mean old Miss Bullock hadn't stolen her fudge bar. Wait a moment... Angela had a brainwave. If all goodies were forbidden, then somewhere in Bracegirdle Hall, there must be a secret stash of them. All she had to do was find it.

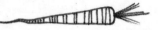

Angela hid behind a pillar. Supper had just finished and Mrs Nicely was lying down upstairs. Heavy footsteps approached. Angela shrank back as Miss Bullock stomped past like a giant.

Angela waited a moment then followed her. Halfway down the corridor Miss Bullock vanished through

a door. Angela read the sign: Staffroom
– private. DO NOT DISTURB!

She peeped through the keyhole.
Inside Miss Bullock was
glugging tea with two
members of staff.

"Anybody peckish?"
she asked.

"Oh, go on then,"
one of the others giggled.

Miss Bullock went to a
cupboard and threw open the door.

Angela's eyes grew big. The shelves
were groaning with goodies – crisps,
biscuits, popcorn, sweets and chocolate.

Miss Bullock handed round biscuits
and bit into a chocolate bar. Angela
gasped – it was *her* fudge bar.

Miss Bullock looked up. "Did you

hear a noise?" Before Angela could move, the door was thrown open. She stood, frozen to the spot.

"What are you doing here?" snapped Miss Bullock.

"I … I just wanted to know if I can go to bed," mumbled Angela.

Miss Bullock pointed to the sign. "Can't you read?" she hissed. "'Do not disturb.' Now go away and don't ask stupid questions!"

BLAM! The door slammed shut and hoots of laughter came from inside. Angela let out a long breath. They would soon see who was stupid.

# Chapter 4

Creep, creep, creep.

Angela tiptoed down the corridor clutching her torch. It was midnight.

"ANGELA!"

Uh oh. She turned round. Her mum's head poked out of their room.

"Where do you think you're going?" she demanded.

*Angela Nicely*

"Just to get some chocolate."

"Don't tell fibs, Angela."

"I'm not, I know where they keep it," said Angela. "There's biscuits and everything."

Mrs Nicely hesitated. She ought to send Angela straight back to bed. On the other hand, she was starving. It was days since she'd tasted anything nicer than a carrot.

"You shouldn't be creeping about at night," she scolded. "What if you're seen?"

"I won't be," promised Angela.

"You had better not," said Mrs Nicely. She lowered her voice. "And don't forget my ginger creams."

Angela padded downstairs and along the silent corridor. No one was about. She opened the staffroom door and

92

slipped inside. Her heart was pounding.
If Miss Bullock caught her, she'd probably
have to swim a million lengths.

Angela shone her torch. There was
the goody cupboard.
She opened the door.
Wowee! It was like
having the key to
a sweet shop.
Quickly, she
began to stuff
the pockets of
her dressing gown.

Ten minutes later, Angela and her mum
sat on the floor. Around them lay sweet
wrappers, crumbs and crisp packets.
It was the greatest midnight feast ever.

"Pass me the ginger creams, please," said Mrs Nicely.

"All gone," said Angela. "Try this toffee popcorn, it's yummy."

Mrs Nicely took a handful. "You're sure no one saw you?"

"Don't worry," said Angela. "They're all in bed…"

CRASH!

Suddenly the door burst open. Miss Bullock stood there with a face as dark as thunder. She had spotted the light under the door as she passed on her nightly patrol.

"WHAT'S GOING ON?" she blazed. "You know the rules, lights out at ten." Her eyes fell on the wrappers and crisp packets. "Where did you get those?"

Angela didn't answer. It was hard to say anything with a mouth full of popcorn.

Miss Bullock narrowed her eyes. "You little sneak," she said. "You raided our cupboard, didn't you? Well, no breakfast for you tomorrow. You'll be doing twenty laps of the grounds."

Angela's heart sank. Please not more laps!

But her mum stood up. "Actually we won't," she said, "because tomorrow morning we're going home."

"Home?" croaked Miss Bullock.

"Yes," replied Mrs Nicely. "I wouldn't stay another day in this horrible place if you paid me."

Angela leaped to her feet. "Does that mean we can go to Splash City?"

Mrs Nicely sighed heavily. "Yes, all right, Angela, as long as you don't—"

Too late, Angela let out an ear-splitting whoop. "YAAAHOOOO!"